Umar and the Bully

Shabana Mir

Illustrated by ASIYA CLARKE

THE ISLAMIC FOUNDATION

To little Umar,
Assad, Shifa, Taha and Izza,
who taught me to love children

© Shabana Mir 1998/1419H

ISBN 0 86037 296 0

MUSLIM CHILDREN'S LIBRARY
UMAR AND THE BULLY
Author: Shabana Mir
Illustrator: Asiya Clarke

Published by
The Islamic Foundation, Markfield Conference Centre, Ratby Lane,
Markfield, Leicester LE67 9SY, United Kingdom
Tel: (01530) 244944 Fax: (01530) 244946
E-Mail: i-foundation@islamic-foundation.org.uk

Quran House, PO Box 30611, Nairobi, Kenya

PMB 3193, Kano, Nigeria

Printed in Great Britain by Ashford Colour Press, Hampshire

Chapter One

A Troubled Boy

U MAR stopped and looked back at the school
gates. The late afternoon sun shone upon
two older boys talking in low voices, huddled
beside the wall. A heavily-built boy handed
something to the other in a clenched fist which he
opened on the palm of the other's hand, so that no
one could see what it was.

Umar knew exactly what it was, and he heard the crackling of a bank-note. The tall boy looked around furtively. Umar turned his head and started walking away slowly. He did not want them to suspect that he knew anything. Then a voice made itself heard inside him, asking: "Are you scared too? Should you be scared?" This voice was familiar to Umar. It was the voice that always came from a mysterious place inside him whenever a problem nagged him.

When he reached the other side of the wide, green field, he sat on the stile to rest for a moment. His forehead was furrowed with lines of worry. He did not like what was going on. It was wrong. He hated knowing about it. Furthermore, he was not sure whether it was right for him to just turn around and walk away without doing anything about it.

A bee hummed as it hovered over the buttercups and chased a squirrel that was scampering about in the afternoon sun. Umar sat there, gazing at the peaceful scene: the green field with the sun pouring down upon it, the buttercups – it was all so lovely and peaceful. It would be even more peaceful when the sun hid its face, the sky became dark and the twinkling stars appeared.

Nature was so beautiful. It felt so right. It radiated so much – why did people have to spoil things? There must be an answer!

Perched on the stile, Umar could not find any answers just yet. He tried to enjoy the scenery, but troubled thoughts kept bubbling to the surface of his mind. Asad's small, frightened face flashed across his thoughts. Oh, no, he did not want to think about that...

3

Chapter Two

A Bully

For Umar, it had all started the day before. He was returning from the gym, happy, hot and tired, when he suddenly heard voices from the changing room. Umar's heart went cold. He heard a hard, angry, cruel voice, followed by a small, stammering one.

"Where's your money today?"

"I... my mummy..."

"Shut up about your mummy! I asked you about your money. Where is it? Stop staring like an idiot. Talk!"

"It's in my bag."

"Go and get it and hurry up! I said, go!"

"It's in my desk in the classroom. Upstairs."

"Listen, Asad, I don't care if it's at the bottom of the swimming pool. I want it, as I told you yesterday. Go and get it! Now!"

Umar heard little footsteps scurrying off, stumbling, and he followed them quietly. The tough-sounding, angry boy was still in the changing room. Umar ran past, feeling a chill in his heart at the thought of the words he had just heard.

He caught up with Asad soon enough because Asad was just a little seven year old, and quite small for his age. He was sobbing, running as fast as his little legs would carry him.

"Asad, stop! What's the matter?" Umar called. Asad jumped with fright when he heard the voice, but when he saw Umar he stopped. He liked Umar, because Umar was kind to the younger children and did not tease or bully them.

"What's the matter?" said Umar again.

Asad didn't want to tell anyone what was going on, but Umar looked so friendly, so kind, that he couldn't stop himself from blurting out the truth.

"Harith wants to take my money," he sobbed, his lower lip quivering as he spoke. "He took it yesterday, too, and I was so tired because I had to walk all the way home, because I couldn't pay for the bus fare and…"

"But that's awful! Didn't you tell anyone? Didn't you tell your teacher right away?"

"I couldn't. Harith said he would give me a black eye

if I told anyone. And anyway, he said if I told anyone, he would say I was lying, and I would just get into trouble for telling lies, because I'm little and he's big."

"That's rubbish," Umar said comfortingly, though he was not sure if it really was. "And he can't hit you, because he'd get into trouble if he did that."

"No, he wouldn't because he would say he hadn't done it. No one tells anyone. Please, Umar – don't ever tell anyone I told you…"

"Don't worry. He doesn't know you told me," Umar answered. Then he looked at Asad thoughtfully and asked, "Asad, what do you mean, no one tells anyone?"

"Don't you know? He takes money from lots of boys in my class, Waseem and Philip and Rashid and Craig and…"

"What?" Umar cried in surprise. "And no one tells anyone? And no one complains?"

"No, of course not! They know he'll hit them harder than he already does if they tell anyone; and you can't get away from Harith when he wants to hit you. He hits you, and David stands next to him, so you can't run away…"

"This is terrible!" Umar exclaimed. "You must tell

your teacher, Asad. He'll take care of you and make sure Harith never takes your money again, or hits or frightens any of the children – ever."

"I'll never, never tell anyone," Asad said, suddenly panic-stricken at the mere thought.

"My teacher doesn't even listen to me, and he doesn't listen to the children if they tell him about Harith and David. He just said to Ghanem, 'Go back to your seat,' when Ghanem told him Harith had stood in his way in the playground and told him to get his money. He doesn't care. He doesn't listen to us. I won't tell him. Never!"

"Oh, no!" Umar sighed, thinking of his own teacher, Mr Fudayl, who was gentle, kind and always willing to listen if you had a problem.

"And yesterday mummy told me off because I said I'd lost my money. Now I'll have to lie again and she'll be angry again and she'll tell my daddy..." Tears started flowing down Asad's cheeks, and he wiped them away quickly with his sleeve and hurried off with his bag.

Umar followed Asad to the changing room and waited outside. He stood perfectly still as Asad went

inside. "Should I go in?" Umar thought. "Should I go in and tell Harith to stop bothering Asad?" He hesitated, and thought, "Oh, no. Am I scared of Harith, just like little Asad?"

"What took you so long?" Harith sounded mean and angry, as if he was clenching his teeth.

But Umar thought, "He sounds nervous. I wonder if he's scared, too?"

"I...I..."Asad stuttered.

"Did you talk to anyone on your way?"

"No!"

"Are you sure?"

"Yes! I swear!"

Umar's heart sank. Now Asad was lying to protect himself. Poor Asad!

"Give me the money! Now, listen!" Harith was talking quickly now. "If you so much as breathe one word about me, or the money, to anyone – anyone at all – I'll break your skinny little arm. This one. You see? Remember Ghanem's bruises? Well, you'll get fifty of those. Understand?"

"Yes, Harith," Asad uttered.

"And stop snivelling! It's nothing new for the kids to hand over their money to the older boys. Lots of them give it. They don't need it anyway. They shouldn't have it. Understand? That's why I take it off them. People would just laugh at you if you made a fuss about your money being taken."

Umar felt a sudden rush of fury as he heard Harith saying such things to Asad. He was telling Asad tales to make the little boy believe he was not so bad after all and what he was doing was normal. He took advantage of the fact that Asad was young and small, and did not know that he was lying.

"Now go to the toilets and wash your face before you go to class. Be here after gym tomorrow!

Remember that! Or I'll remind you at the tuck shop at break! Let's go, David!"

Umar slipped off to class, his mind heavy, his heart beating hard and fast. So David was with Harith. Maybe that was why Harith was being so nasty. Well, he was nasty anyway, but David made him worse. When they were together, they were not afraid of doing wrong things. They stood at the gates and cracked jokes about the others as they walked past. They frightened the younger boys and called them bad names.

As Umar sat at his desk, staring glumly out of the window, he watched Harith pass by. Harith had broad shoulders and large hands, and he wore an ear-ring in his left ear. Most of the boys were frightened of him, and everyone tried to keep out of his way, even if they were not willing to admit it.

Many pupils said he smoked cigarettes, and that David had started smoking since they had become friends. David was skinny, with a thin, pinched face and hawk-like eyes. He was rude, but in a spiteful, low-voiced way, so he did not get into fights unless Harith was around. He was pale and not very strong, but he was always with Harith, so everyone was afraid of him, too. The other boys whispered secretly about how cruel they were, and how they would steal things from the shops. David was clever but he spent a lot of time hanging around with Harith and his marks had dropped.

Chapter Three

Good Advice

Umar thought about all these things as he walked home across the field. He remembered how Harith had handed David his share of the money at the school gates, and how Asad had walked home crying.

They had taken Asad's money. Also, they had made him tell lies, even to his mother. They had done the same, and worse, to other boys. It was all so very, very wrong...

Umar was so preoccupied with his thoughts that he had difficulty concentrating on his homework. He had to talk to someone about this bullying. Something had to be done to stop them. Eventually, he decided to tell Muhammad. Muhammad was a good friend of his, a good boy. Umar trusted him. Muhammad was sensible, and he would not spoil things by telling the wrong people.

Muhammad listened in silence to the story, worried as well.

"... and I decided to tell you because I don't know what to do. I mean, I could just keep quiet about it

and not tell anyone, as the others are doing. But that wouldn't be right, would it?" Umar said on finishing his story.

"No," Muhammad replied in a resolute tone. "We're not supposed to do that. If something is wrong, we're supposed to change it, and make it right."

Umar was happy and relieved to hear Muhammad say "we". It meant that Muhammad would share his problem and that he would not just tell him to ignore it. It was good to have a friend like Muhammad.

However, it was one thing to accept that they ought to right the wrong, but quite another to solve the problem. Umar and Muhammad fell silent for a few minutes and thought hard.

"Muhammad, are you a little scared of Harith?" Umar began.

Muhammad said cautiously. "Er… well…"

"Because I think I am," Umar said.

"Oh, yes. I am, too," Muhammad admitted. "Everyone is, I think."

"But we shouldn't be."

"I suppose not," Muhammad agreed. "But they do hit the younger children, you know. And they're always together, Harith and David."

"But think of the whole school against just two boys! Isn't it a bit silly?"

"I hadn't thought of it that way."

"And you know, Muhammad, there's another thing. I think he's scared, too."

"Who?"

"Harith! Yes, I mean it! I was listening to him today and he sounded so nervous. I think if someone – just someone – faced him, and stood up to him, and answered him back and showed him he wasn't scared of him, that might teach him a lesson."

"Time to pray," Muhammad's father called them from the sitting room. "Are you two boys going to join us for prayer?" he asked.

Umar and Muhammad went into the sitting room where Muhammad's father had already spread out the prayer mats. Umar stood between Muhammad and his elder brother Abdullah. Shayma, Muhammad's elder sister, prayed with them, too.

When the prayer had finished, Umar thought, "This home is as peaceful as the buttercup field. Allah can make everything calm. He is strong, the strongest of all, much stronger than either Harith or David. Besides, they're cruel and nasty, but Allah is kind, the kindest of all."

Umar whispered, "Dear Allah, You know everything about Asad, Harith and David. Asad is so scared. Well, I know it's wrong to rob people, hit and frighten them, and I do want to stop them. But You know –

I'm a little scared, too. And I know I'm not supposed to be scared, because a Muslim isn't, and he's supposed to stop bad things from happening. Please don't think badly of me for being frightened, but help me do the right thing. I don't know what to do. Please help me and Asad. And help Muhammad to help me, too."

As he was rolling up the prayer mat, he noticed Abdullah looking at him with a smile in his eyes. A faint smile. Umar decided to talk to him, just a little bit. He would not tell him the whole story, though.

"Abdullah."

"Yes?"

"Can I ask you something?" Umar began.

"Of course."

"A Muslim is supposed to be brave, isn't he?" Umar asked.

"Yes, he is," Abdullah answered.

Instantly Shayma piped up, "...or she."

Abdullah laughed and said, "Yes, or she. Why, Umar? Is something bothering you?"

"What if a Muslim is scared?" Umar asked.

"Oh, that's all right," Abdullah replied reassuringly.

"Is it?" Umar asked, relieved.

"Yes, it's all right to be scared in your heart sometimes. But we still trust Allah and know that the strongest person and the most ferocious animal can't do anything to hurt us if Allah protects us. So what we do is what Allah wants us to do."

"I see…"

"And we ask Him to protect us from everything harmful, and He does. So we trust, love and obey Him, no matter what happens, and He's pleased with us."

Chapter Four

A Fine Example

Shayma was rolling up her prayer mat. She was nine years older than Umar and had known him since he was a baby. She turned and said, "Umar, remember when you were born?"

"Well, no!"

"No, I don't mean that," she laughed. "I mean, you know when you were born, your parents had already chosen your name. Do you know why they chose Umar?"

"Because they wanted me to be brave like Syedina Umar al-Farooq," replied Umar.

He thought of how he had stayed outside the changing room today and felt uneasy.

"And he was courageous in doing whatever Allah and the Prophet said to do. If anyone did anything wrong, they'd be afraid of Umar."

"Yes, Umar was brave, but he wasn't only brave. He was very kind to the poor and the weak as well," Abdullah said. "He was like a rock when he faced people who did wrong, and he was as gentle as a lamb when he faced the needy."

"Once there was a famine and people didn't have enough to eat," Shayma said. "And Umar promised himself that he wouldn't taste meat, butter or milk until the people had enough to eat."

"Daddy says he used to walk the streets at night in disguise to find out if anyone was in need, so he could help them," Muhammad said. "He did, didn't he, Shayma?"

"Yes, Muhammad," Shayma answered. "And have you heard about the woman who didn't have anything to give to her children?"

"Oh, yes," Umar exclaimed. "He was walking

through the streets one night when he saw a woman
cooking something, while her children were crying
beside her. Umar asked the woman why they were
crying, and she tearfully explained that they were
crying for food, but she didn't have any at all. She
was cooking stones in a pot, so that the children
would think food was being prepared."

"Umar was terribly upset," Shayma said. "He
rushed back to Madina that very moment. He
collected flour, dates and some other things and took

them all the way back to the family himself. His slave wanted to take them for him, but he wanted to do it himself, because it was his responsibility. And while the woman cooked the food, he kept the children busy playing. Yet, he was the caliph of the great Muslim country!"

"Didn't she know who he was?" Umar asked. "Wasn't she embarrassed because the caliph himself came carrying bags of flour and dates for her?"

"Oh, she didn't know," Shayma replied with a smile. "His actions were so simple that you couldn't tell he was a powerful ruler. None of the rich clothes and bodyguards that you see nowadays! But when the children had finished eating and he was about to leave, she thanked him and said, 'Really, you ought to be the caliph instead of Umar!' I suppose he didn't want to embarrass her by telling her who he really was!"

Chapter Five

About Responsibility

When the story was over, everyone was quiet for a while, deep in their own thoughts. Umar, especially, was thinking hard. Eventually he broke the silence.

"Why did Umar feel so responsible for other people?"

"Well, for one thing, Umar was the ruler, the caliph. He used to say that if a dog died by the River Tigris, he would be accountable for it to Allah," Abdullah explained. "But you don't have to be a caliph or a king to be responsible for others."

"What do you mean?" Muhammad asked.

"Well, you know, we're all responsible for at least someone," Shayma answered. "Not more than we can manage, but we should take care of those people we can help."

"Like... who?"

"Like mummy and daddy, they're responsible for us in many, many ways. They have to be good to us, take care of us, try and give us food and clothes, and also educate us to be good human beings, as much as they can," Shayma said. "And, for instance, I'm responsible for Muhammad and Abdullah, too, in a way, because I'm their elder sister. I try and make sure they're happy, and if anything is bothering them, I try and help them. And Abdullah is  responsible for Muhammad, in the same way."

"Some people don't care about others," Umar said thoughtfully. "It's as if they don't have any time for other people. Some friends behave like that, and some teachers."

"Yes, but that's not the way Allah wants us to be. He doesn't want us to be selfish and small-minded, thinking only of ourselves. He wants us to be good to as many people as possible – and not just people but animals, plants, the environment..."

"Is Mr Fudayl responsible for us, too?" Umar asked.

"Mr Fudayl's your teacher, isn't he?" Abdullah said.

"Yes, he must teach you well, and must help you whenever you need help, and teach you to be obedient to Allah."

"But what if someone bullied me and I told Mr Fudayl?" Umar said. "What if I told him, but he didn't care, or he just didn't do anything about it. Would that be all right?"

"No, really, he shouldn't do that," Abdullah replied. "A teacher should do his best to make sure no one bullies anyone else. He's responsible for that, too."

Asad and Muhammad looked at each other. Asad's teacher hadn't helped Asad at all. That had spoiled things a lot.

"When I become a teacher," Umar said firmly, "I'll be kind to the children, and I'll protect them from anyone who tries to bully them. What use is it being grown-up and strong if you're not going to protect the little ones, and if you're not going to stop the bullies?"

"Oh, you don't have to wait till you're grown-up, Umar," Abdullah said, standing up. "You're a brave boy and you're a Muslim. A Muslim has nothing to be afraid of. You can help those younger than yourself, even now."

"I must go," Shayma also got up. "I've got homework to do. Assalaam alaikum, everybody."

"Walaikum salaam," they replied. Umar and Muhammad remained in the sitting room.

"Umar," Muhammad spoke first. "Did you hear all that?"

"I did," Umar replied. "Are you thinking what I'm thinking?"

"I'm thinking about being responsible for others," Muhammad said.

"So am I," Umar said. "Are we responsible for Asad? He is small enough, really."

"I think so, yes," Muhammad answered. "Because

he's in trouble, and then he's little. I think so, yes."

"So do I," Umar agreed. "He's too scared to protect himself, and in a way I can understand, you know, because his teacher won't help him. We're lucky to be older and bigger than he is and to have Mr Fudayl. I think we ought to try and help."

"It is his teacher's responsibility, though, isn't it?"

"Well, yes," Umar answered thoughtfully. "But just because the poor thing doesn't have a helpful teacher, he shouldn't have to suffer like this."

"You're right. And I don't want to be like his teacher. He may not have asked us for help, of course, but we know he needs it."

"Right, then," Umar said firmly. "I'll see Asad tomorrow insh'Allah, and ask him if he has told anyone yet."

"Right," Muhammad agreed. "Then we'll decide what to do."

Chapter Six

The Victim

It was Thursday. Umar was going to his science class when he came across Asad sitting on the stairs looking rather lost and lonely. Umar stopped and said, "Oh, there you are, Asad. I was looking for you. How is everything?"

Asad did not answer at first, then he whispered, "What?"

30

"You know," Umar said, upset at seeing Asad so quiet, "with Harith and David."

Asad looked around and his chin trembled.

"What's the matter?" Umar said, worried. "Did they take your money again?"

Asad nodded silently.

"Asad, why don't you speak? Nobody's around."

Asad looked timidly at Umar. "I stole mummy's money," he said guiltily.

"You what?" Umar said, shocked. "Did they tell you to do that?"

Asad nodded.

"I know, and I'm so scared at night because I've been stealing, that I might die and go to hell and..."

"Oh, no, Asad. You're too little," Umar answered, upset because Asad was so frightened. "Oh, no, I wish there was a grown-up to take care of this. But you mustn't steal money. You shouldn't have..."

Asad looked over his shoulder, and then Umar saw that he had a bruise under his chin, and another on his right cheek. Nasty, dark bruises.

"How did you get those bruises, Asad?"

Silence. Asad's chin was trembling again. A tear slipped down his cheek.

"They hit you, didn't they?"

31

It was true. The terror in Asad's face was something Umar could remember from when he was a little boy, too. Suddenly Asad looked up. Harith was coming down the stairs. Asad stood up and ran up the stairs to the toilets. Harith passed by Umar, and Umar felt a sudden surge of anger. Anger because Asad was little and defenceless, and Harith was such a big bully. Umar felt more angry than afraid. But he did not do anything. Not just yet, he thought. Before he did anything, he must talk to Muhammad and plan things, otherwise he might mess things up. Then Asad

and he would end up in bigger trouble than before.

"... And if things carry on like this, this bullying and robbing and stealing will go on and on and on..." said Umar, as he finished telling Muhammad his story.

"... And Harith will go on bullying and frightening and hitting people. And, you know, some day one of the little children will grow up to become a kind of Harith, just because they were so frightened of Harith at school."

"Shall we tell Asad's teacher then?" Muhammad suggested.

"No use," Umar replied. "Asad and we would get into trouble. No, I know Mr Fudayl isn't Asad's teacher, and it's not really his responsibility in a way – but I think he'd care about it. You know, just like we're worried about Asad even though we're not his teachers or his parents. We just ought to feel for him. Allah wants us to."

"All right, then, we'll tell Mr Fudayl," Muhammad murmured thoughtfully. "Harith and David might get us anyway."

"Maybe," Umar admitted after a moment's silence.

33

Chapter Seven

A Matter of Trust

That night, as Umar lay in bed, he looked up at the stars from his little window. Asad must be in bed, too. Umar remembered that when he was upset, he sometimes cried silently in bed until he fell asleep.

Perhaps Asad was crying even now. Umar turned over restlessly. It was all Harith's fault. Why did people have to be so nasty and cruel? Why couldn't they try and be good to other people instead? Didn't Harith also find it horrid to be hated by so many people at school?

Anyway, it had happened now, and something had to be done about it.

"All right, Allah, this is it," Umar whispered. "I'm sorry I was scared before, but I'm sure you'll understand. I didn't protect Asad before, but I'll do it now. I'm not as scared as I was before, though. You know, let me not be frightened at all! Not in the least. I know You'll protect me as I'm trying to protect Asad. The difference is, I'm scared, and You're not scared of anyone or anything. You can take care of everyone. Tomorrow I'll tell Mr Fudayl about Harith and Asad.

Just make me strong, Allah! And make sure Harith doesn't hurt me or Asad – or Muhammad, because he'll be with us, too!"

Then he thought, "Well, what if he does hit me?" And he decided, "Right. This is the right thing to do, and I'll just do it. I'll trust You and I don't care what happens."

Tired yet restless, Umar turned over and tried to sleep.

35

Chapter Eight

A Brave Boy

The next day, Mr Fudayl did not teach them the whole morning. They had maths with another teacher instead. Umar was somewhat nervous, but he had told Muhammad his plan. Muhammad had agreed, and they waited expectantly for the afternoon.

After lunch, Umar was going upstairs to the classroom with Muhammad. They were talking about the geography class they had just had. At that moment, Muhammad tugged Umar's sleeve and said, "Look!"

Umar looked up and saw Asad following Harith down the stairs. Harith was saying something as Asad hung his head submissively.

"He must be taking him somewhere to get more money out of him," Umar said angrily. "It's not fair. Poor Asad – look at how scared he looks."

"Let's fetch Mr Fudayl," Muhammad suggested.

"That'll take a few minutes, and then we won't know where they've gone," Umar said quickly. "We can't let Harith rob Asad again. I'll go after them."

"But, Umar," Muhammad protested, "we'll hurry

and fetch Mr Fudayl. You can't go, Harith might..."

"You go and get him," Umar said, "I'm going after them."

"Umar!" Muhammad began...

"I've got to help Asad now," Umar replied, "I said I would."

Umar followed Asad and Harith to the playground. It was deserted now, and they were the only boys there. Harith had not seen him yet. Asad was looking down at the ground, so he could hardly see anything but his own shoes.

"All right, how much have you got today?" Harith turned threateningly towards Asad. Asad mumbled something...

"Speak up, you little brat! How much?" Harith grabbed Asad's shoulder, and shook him hard. Asad cried out.

"Don't touch him, Harith!" Umar heard himself say. "Don't you touch him again! He hasn't hurt you – why are you bothering him?"

Harith turned and stared at Umar, totally amazed. No one talked to him like that. He looked hard at Umar, and though Umar half-expected Harith to hit him, he just looked him straight in the eye. To his surprise, Harith shrugged his shoulders and looked away. "Get lost, Umar. This is none of your business, you hear?"

"It's my business, now," Umar said boldly. "I know you've been bothering Asad, and the other children, too. I know all about you. You stop taking his money, or you'll be in big trouble."

Harith stared, his eyes wide and bulging. He turned on Asad and grabbed him roughly by his arm.

"So you've been lying to Umar, have you? What did I tell you? Umar, you go away. Now. You hear? If you don't go, I'll give you such a black eye that'll last for months. Just get lost. David will be here soon."

"You're afraid, aren't you, Harith?" Umar replied,

trying to calm his quickening heart-beat. "That's
why you need David around. And I don't care, I
won't let you hurt Asad or take his money again.
You made him steal his mother's money, too. Hey,
I told you not to touch him. Don't touch him,
Harith…"

Harith was stretching out his hand to slap Asad.
Umar jumped in front of him and pulled Asad out of
the way, facing Harith himself. Harith raised his
hand threateningly above Umar when, suddenly, a
larger hand grasped Harith's.

Chapter Nine

Friends in Need

"That's enough, Harith – the game's over now,"
Mr Fudayl said.

Harith and Umar looked up, confused.

"You are not to use violence on each other. Now, I
want you to come with me this very moment, and we
shall speak to the headmaster about your activities. I'm
sure he'll be very interested. Umar, Muhammad and
Asad, I want you three to come, too, but after about
fifteen minutes. We will speak to Harith alone first.
Come along, then. Walk fast!"

Shocked into silence, Harith went off with Mr Fudayl.
He could not deny anything, because Mr Fudayl had

heard some of his conversation with Umar. He was looking around in bewilderment, wondering what to do next, and looking for David, but David was nowhere to be seen. As Umar was staring at them, he realised that Muhammad was speaking.

"I fetched Mr Fudayl as fast as I could," he said. "We weren't too late, were we, Umar? Nothing else happened, did it? I didn't know where you were, but I asked Mr Fudayl to run so we would find you quick enough, before you had a fight. Umar, you were

very brave, you know, the way you protected Asad. Are you all right?"

"Yes, I'm fine," Umar answered, sitting down slowly. "For a moment I thought there was going to be a fight, but I'm glad there wasn't one."

"Gosh! Were you scared? You must have been."

"I don't know. Before it happened, I suppose I was scared even of talking to Harith, but when it came to it, I was ready for it. It's odd, isn't it?"

"He was very brave," Asad said admiringly. "He was big and brave and he didn't let Harith hit me."

"Yes, well, he won't bother you any more," Muhammad said.

"What did Mr Fudayl say would happen?" Umar asked.

"Mr Fudayl said the headmaster had already heard about Harith bullying the younger children, but when he asked them, they were all too scared to say anything, so they just said that nothing had happened," Muhammad said. "Mr Fudayl explained that now someone was ready to speak out, the headmaster would have proof, and he could do something about him."

"That's funny, isn't it?" Umar commented. "Even one or two people can make a difference to so many others. Just because we spoke out, everyone can be safe from Harith now."

"It's good we found out about being responsible, isn't it?" Muhammad said excitedly.

"Yes, but I felt stronger because you stood by me, Muhammad," Umar said, appreciatively. "And then you brought Mr Fudayl just in time."

"Yes, but you were the brave one," Muhammad said. "You followed Harith so he wouldn't hurt Asad ever again."

43

Chapter Ten

Friends Indeed

That night, watching the clouds shimmer in the moonlight as he lay in bed, Umar leaned his elbow on the window sill.

"Everyone thinks I'm brave, Allah," he said, "but I know that You made me brave, because I asked You. Thank You, and thank You for a friend like Muhammad."

After a moment's thought he added, "And thank You for being my friend. And let me always be brave and kind so that I can help others in difficult situations. Just like Hadhrat Umar," he said, turning over and falling fast asleep.